Gideon Elliot

The Recruiter

Gay Romance Erotica

WARNING

This book contains sexually explicit scenes and adult language. It may be considered offensive to some readers. This book is for sale to adults ONLY.

Please store your files wisely where they cannot be accessed by underage readers.

* * * * * * * * * * * * * * * * * * *

WANT FREE COPIES OF MY BOOKS?
Just visit my blog and download free copies of my books:
http://gideon-elliot.awesomeauthors.org/gideon-elliot/

About the Publisher
4Fun Publishing, a member of **BLVNP Incorporated**, 340 S. Lemon #6200, Walnut CA 91789, info@blvnp.com / legal@blvnp.com
NOTE: Due to the highly emotional reaction of some people to works of erotic fiction, any email sent to the above address that contains foul language or religious references is automatically deleted by our anti-spam software and will not be seen. All other communications are welcome.

DISCLAIMER
Please don't be stupid and kill yourself. This book is a work of FICTION. Do not try any new sexual practice that you find in this book. It is fiction and not to be confused with reality. Neither the author nor the publisher or its associates assume any responsibility for any loss, injury, death or legal consequences resulting from acting on the contents in this book. Every character in this book is over 18 years of age. The author's opinions are not to be construed as the opinions of the publisher. The material in this book is for entertainment purposes ONLY. Enjoy.

The Recruiter
Gay Romance Erotica

By: Gideon Elliot

© **Gideon Elliot 2015**
ISBN: 978-1-62761-403-0

Chapter 1

The numbers were bad, the scandal was worse, the colonel was apoplectic, the headlines were grim, the war was a mess. Congress was concerned. The president said he did not see any reason to worry about anything. In public the White House press spokesman was upbeat and calm; in private, things were different.

A secret e-mail from someone in Rumsfeld's office to the colonel said, Get those fucking numbers up or you'll be going down. And do it without making a horse's ass out of the army.

Someone from Cheney's office was overheard saying between bites of sushi, "The vice-president said that if those cocksuckers don't know how to get boys and girls into uniforms, they should be wearing diapers and sucking their mothers' tits instead of carrying weapons and wearing the uniforms of the armed services."

* * *

Scotty Mason had a lousy headache. He'd had it all day. He'd had it yesterday. It wasn't going away. Neither was his unfilled quota. Neither were the stories about what recruiters were doing to fill their quotas. Neither was the growing disgust with the war and the government.

He would have preferred to be in a combat unit sticking close to his buddies, sharing the adrenaline rush, focusing together on one thing, rather than to be waylaying these boys in the mall and suffering humiliation after defeat after humiliation.

He came back, nevertheless, after each blow, after each failure, taller than before, crisper than ever.

"Gentlemen you need to talk to me about putting some purpose in your life," he'd say, and some bright-eyed smart-aleck who needed a haircut and a belt for his pants would answer back, "Hey, man, I got a purpose. It's keeping out of the clutches of guys like you."

It shouldn't have gotten to him, but all through the day and every night, sentences like that just kept on banging around inside his head, clogging his memory. And the faces of the boys he saw, he couldn't get them out of his head. All those young, sweet faces saying "No" to him! All those bodies churning with life, who could have been his buddies, retracting from him! Or worse -- meeting him with taunts and defiance. Oh, when they taunted him, when they showed that defiant attitude, did he ever want to take those cunts and bend them to his will like they'd never been bent.

* * *

"Name's Scott. What's yours?" he said, hand extended, approaching a guy who was a more likely looking recruit than the average hippie faggots he had to comb through. He was well built, stood straight, dressed conservatively and with style. He was looking' good. And he was by himself.

"Derek."

"Cool, Derek. You look like a man with a plan, a guy with a purpose, a dude who's above the crowd. We should talk."

"About what?" Derek answered, freeing his hand from the soldier's grasp.

"How 'bout your future?"

"What about my future?"

"Have you ever thought what it's gonna be?"

Derek almost smiled, but otherwise, he did not answer.

"I thought so," Scott said, riffing his way through the ambiguity.

"Let's sit down and talk. Hungry?"

Derek shook his head.

"Here's the plan, Derek," the sergeant said, biting into a hamburger and taking a sip of cherry soda.

"You sign with me... You sure you don't want a burger, eh? Maybe just a soda?"

"I'm sure."

"...for two years and you've got...tastes good... sure?"

Derek nods without a word.

"Ok. But if you change your mind....So you've got four years in college, an extra five Gs to spend, and a feeling about yourself that no amount of money can buy and no one can ever take away. Now that sounds good, huh?"

"Not so good," Derek said quietly.

"What'd you say?" Scott stopped chewing to ask.

"Not so good," Derek repeated, no louder.

"Not good!"

"No."

"How's that?"

"I'm not into it."

"I don't believe you."

"Suit yourself."

"I mean, come on, a smart dude like you. All you can say is I'm not into it?"

"I'm not."

"So why you here talking to me?"

"You're the one who's talking."

"But you're still here listening, Derek. Why you sitting here with me if you aren't interested, dude?"

"To see how you operate."

"To see how I operate?"

"Yeah."

"Just like that."

"Uh-huh."

'You jerkin' my chain, man?"

"You feel like I am?"

This was getting difficult. Scott took a breath and then resumed.

"So what do you think about what I had to say, Derek, about my offer?"

He was working hard to keep the edge out of his voice. This fish wasn't off his hook yet, even if he thought he was free and just teasing. He wasn't going to let him get away. The kid was too cool by half, too cool for his own good. He'd take some knocking down. But it was a good challenge. He had backbone.

If I can break him, I'll own him, Scott thought. That, he felt in his deepest gut. This kid was a prize among a lot of losers.

From outside, it didn't look like it; but inside the space that hung between them, there was a struggle going on between two minds for which one was going to be dominant. Each of them knew that they'd sat down together with the purpose of tackling the other one.

"C'mon, Derek, what can you say against what I just told you?"

"Wrong question," Derek said in the same low tone but with a direct and steady gaze that made Scott uncomfortable: what the fuck was that supposed to mean? And, hey, he was the one who was supposed to be doing the heavy eye-balling.

"Wrong question?" Scott repeated trying to hide his confusion, rifling through his mind for interview techniques he'd been taught in training.

"Yeah."

You needed a can opener with this guy, he thought, but restrained himself from expressing his annoyance.

"Ok, I'll bite. What's the right question, Derek?"

"That's your job."

"I've met some tight assholes before," Sgt. Mason said, losing it, "but..."

Derek stood.

"Hey wait, buddy. Sit down. No offense."

But Derek turned and started walking away.

"Yo, Derek, buddy. The conversation was just getting started. Don't split."

But when the kid didn't turn back and Scotty was left staring at a solidly well-built American guy with an attitude as hard and as polished as an industrial diamond getting away from him, he pushed his tray to the center of the table and stood up and took a few quick steps and was walking out of the mall alongside his prey.

"You got something to tell me, Derek, and you're not saying."

"No."

"How come you're turning down my offer, Derek?"

"How come you're following me?"

"You know you made a commitment, Derek, when you sat down with me, which isn't so easy to get out of, dude."

"What commitment did you make?"

Derek turned his head when he said it, and again looked steadily into Scott's eyes, and it was unnerving to him. He was as good as they come at holding another man's glance without flinching, and making the other guy blink first. But Derek wasn't trying to stare him down or lock his gaze. It was an open look the likes of which Mason had never seen before. And it confused him, threw him off balance. Derek's eyes were soft.

Try out-staring the blue sky on a spring day.

But Scott caught himself just in time.

"Why don't you come back to my office with me and I'll show you. My car's right over there in the lot."

"No," Derek said.

"Don't you ever say anything but 'no', Derek? You are one negative dude. You know that, Derek?"

Derek shrugged, didn't say anything, and just kept walking, indifferent to his companion, somehow giving Scott the feeling that he was not at all his companion, that, in fact, he did not really exist, as far as the boy was concerned.

And this, even more than his fierce desire to lock the boy into a contract is what kept him going, pushing at the boy; trying to get Derek to acknowledge him, to feel the volume of his presence, its solidity, to act like he was there and that he took up a certain amount of space and had weight. He could have dealt with resistance.

* * *

Mason got out of his uniform and stood in front of the mirror, alone in the apartment he shared with two other recruiters, looking at himself, naked, the no frills, stripped-down version. It wasn't so long ago he was a carefree college jock who took everything easy and for whom things, in fact, came easy: athletics, academics, friendships, girls… Girls, Christ, they were all over him. It was ok, but it never lived up to the feelings he'd imagined when he'd talked to other guys about girls.

He still had the body, it was even buffer, but he saw something new in his eyes, something tighter, something frantic. Eagerness had been replaced by anxiety; spunkiness, by guile. And his hair, he had plenty of it and it was well-groomed, but it didn't have that spring-foliage-after-the-rain look it once had.

He had gone into ROTC because he thought it was a good idea, a good thing to do because the head of ROTC had given a talk in the locker room and fired up a lot of guys on the football team with a mix of promises and warnings and some A-1 videos of heavy dudes, explosive action, and attention-grabbing technology.

He was a hypnotic speaker and made them feel the need in their lives for a sense of purpose, to commit themselves to something bigger than themselves, greater than themselves, and that only by doing that would they be able to be really big men who not only could take command of themselves but could take command of others.

The guys on the team sat there in the locker room, powerful guys, half-dressed and sprawled out, comfortable in their bodies, confident in their domain, and excited by the comradeship they were feeling around a common mission.

So it wasn't even weird, it did not seem weird, that afterwards Scotty went down to The Slammer with a couple of the other guys and shared a few pitchers of beer and talked about a great future, and it did not seem weird that they threw their arms around each other afterwards as they walked back to Mike Finnegan's apartment and stripped down to their underwear there and popped some more cans of beer and started rough-housing, and it did not seem weird when they got hard cocks.

They knew they were men and they lit cigars and started strutting around clownishly showing off how big they were, and one thing led to another, and soon they were getting each other off, and not just with their hands, but with their beer-rubbery mouths they were working each other's' cocks, too, until the spray from their cocks and the foam from the beer mixed together in one blinding froth.

Mason got a boner thinking about it, and the whole shooting gallery was replaced in his mind by an image of that prick, Derek, standing in front of him, at attention, in his uniform, calling him Sir.

Chapter 2

Scotty Mason woke with a bad headache -- again. It wouldn't go away. It was tormenting him. He'd had it for weeks. But today it was fierce. With each throb, he felt a spurt of real anger. He sat up and pulled a crumpled cigarette from the torn pack by the bedside and let it hang unlit in his mouth.

His hands turned into fists as he thought about it. But there was nothing to do. The bastard had out-smarted him.

He lit the match he was holding and put it to the bent edge of the cigarette.

The guy at the mall yesterday who got away, that fucking Derek.

He wanted to take that smartass kid and slam him against the wall, and hold him there while he taught him how it was to show some respect to your superiors.

He wanted to hold him against the wall by his throat and watch the kid quail.

He pulled himself out of bed, sat on the edge, took a few last drags on the cigarette and stubbed it out in the butt-filled ash-tray on the nightstand.

There was a thunderstorm and lightning outside, and rain was pelting the window panes.

"Fuck, shit, fuck," he grumbled as a hard stream of piss hit the water in the toilet bowl. "What a lousy day to have to go out fishing."

He was way below his quota for the last three months, and every day he had to put up with being chewed out by the colonel. Stupid motherfucker, he didn't even know what it was like out there.

Resistance was growing on the kids like a fungus.

He was alone for the weekend. Ryan was visiting his parents; Quincy, his girlfriend in Dallas.

He switched on the TV as he made a cup of instant coffee. He stood in front of it as he drank the insipid brew, still only in his khaki skivvies, mindlessly scratching his balls and cursing at the reporter who was highlighting the story. Two recruiters in Washington State got an autistic kid to sign up. Then they tried to tough it out while his family, the press, and finally his congressman made a holy stink about it.

He put his coffee cup down and lit another cigarette. They were accusing the recruiters of strong arm tactics and then knocking what the troops were doing in Iraq on top of it.

He knew he had to calm down. He had to be positive.

He crushed the cigarette, showered and shaved and got into his uniform and pulled himself together.

He stood in front of the mirror and saluted himself.

"Mason!" he said.

"Yes, Sir," he answered.

* * *

A good start for the day was another cup of coffee and a donut inside the mall. No chance for a cigarette here. Saturday morning, the place has to be swarming with possibilities. Maybe even that prick Derek would show up.

He'd get in his face and not let him go this time. That was one kid he wanted to catch and sign up.

If he knew the kid's last name, he'd give him a call. Maybe one of those other cunts who hung out at the mall would know it.

He shut and opened his eyes, rubbed them, and then opened his hand and rubbed the sides of his face by the bone of the eye sockets with extended thumb and forefinger. He pulled himself together. He couldn't let himself zone out over his coffee. And he couldn't let himself keep thinking about Derek like this -- he was working. Yeah, but the thing with Derek was about work.

Mason looked around as if studying the mall's architecture.

A bunch of young guys in baggy clothes stopped at the electronics store and messed around with each other, leaping and landing and yelping as they commented on the devices in the window.

He felt defeated before he began.

"Gentleman," he said, and despite his apprehension, he approached the group.

"You look like a team on the beam that wants to see some action."

"Oh, no," one of them in a sleeveless shirt and a backwards baseball cap groaned, "team on the beam." He walked away with a slouch.

"We got our action, Dude. We don't want your kind of action," another one said, a hippie with an earring. Or may just a faggot. What was the difference, anyway?

"I see how you're checking out all that equipment," Mason went on ignoring them, trying to find a hook. "Well you ought to check out the army because the army's got some high tech stuff that'll make the stuff you're looking at in the window seem like black and white television."

But the kids weren't biting. He found himself in the ridiculous position of following after them. "Gentlemen," he said, trying to get their attention, "Dudes."

But they had no interest in paying attention to him, and as long as they did not get caught by him, he couldn't make them.

An army recruiter has mystical power. He is an archetype. He is the force that makes the landscape dangerous, the agent of a power that can transform your world from an open and free place where you belong to yourself to a lock-up where you belong to someone else, someone who can dispose of you as he will, even to the death. The army recruiter can be the agent of death, the lingering Erlking beckoning. He invites both defiance and surrender.

The more political among the kids organized demonstrations against the recruiters. But most of the kids kept their distance. Recruiters are dangerous.

And then there are those kids that get caught. Some think they want what the recruiters are selling. Others get bamboozled by forces beyond their comprehension.

* * *

Standing in the center of the atrium, facing a store that sold leather fashions, Mason felt uncomfortable being himself. It wasn't like anything he had ever felt before. Properly, then he should not have known what it meant to feel the way he did. It ought to be an unidentifiable feeling. But it wasn't. It was a distinct feeling that told him he was uncomfortable being himself. He knew it.

He shook his head as if he wanted to shake such thoughts out of his head -- or as if he wanted to shake himself free of himself.

He needed to sit down someplace, to rest. He felt nausea.

In the Men's room, in a large stall with a toilet and a baby diaper changing table, he sat and bent forward and clasped his head in his hands.

"This is very dangerous," he said to himself in a panic at his confusion. "Not following orders is insubordination."

He stood. He became dizzy. He opened the door to the stall knowing he had to get out. He fell and hit the floor.

A kid on his way to pick up tickets for a Neil Young concert heard something as he passed the Men's room. Inside he found a soldier face down on the bathroom tile. Luckily Reese, the security guy, was right there, and he called the emergency squad. Mason was coming to, but was disoriented, had trouble speaking.

The transient ischemic attack was minor. To the extent that such things can ever be considered as not serious, it was not serious. But it was a warning. Mason knew by an intuition that had never before graced him. He was a tight fit of anger, all throughout his body. Everything about him was clenched.

* * *

"You're no good to us," the colonel said. "I have to be honest with you."

"I guess I'm not much good to myself, either," Mason said.

"That's no way to talk."

"Yes, sir," Mason said, falling back on the only prop he knew, the discipline of taking orders.

"No, no, Mason. You can't tough this one out. If you take my advice, you go get some counseling. It's rough out there. You'll get a medical discharge, no disgrace."

The colonel pushed back on his chair and stood up. The meeting was over.

* * *

No disgrace! Ha! It was a big disgrace, and he knew it, and they knew it, and everybody knew it. But everybody was acting like nothing had happened, that a dream had not been shattered. The only thing he had ever wanted, really wanted, was to be among other guys like himself, to be one of a band of brothers sharing a noble purpose and bound together by their dedication to their duty and to each other. Instead of that he had to go cruising malls getting shit on by hippies, not even with a partner, like most guys, because there was a shortage of recruiters here. And what did it get him? Shit from little motherfuckers like Derek and condescension from his superior officers. And now he was nothing, absolutely nothing.

So for the first couple of weeks, he totally went to seed. He was ashamed to go outside. He spent days in bed. He didn't wash or shave. His hair grew long and shaggy. When he finally was ready to go out again, he didn't recognize himself when he looked in the bathroom mirror.

"So much the better," he thought. "No risk anyone else will either."

He had the urge to drive over to the mall; so much had happened there. He needed to look around once more, to say good-bye.

How strange suddenly to need to say good-by to a place you never wanted to be.

Then, spontaneously, despite himself, it came to him even though he did not want it to, did not want to know what he realized he knew. It was not about the mall or about who he had been or what he had been doing. It was only one thing that mattered to him, one thing only that he wanted: it was that fucking Derek.

He wanted to see that guy in uniform, standing at attention, saluting him.

That prick had penetrated him and he couldn't do anything about it. If he had only gotten Derek to sign!

He stood by the soda machine looking at the floor and shaking his head. When he looked up he saw a bunch of kids across the way – he recognized some of them -- looking at him, noticing him, unable to be sure they were seeing what they thought they were seeing.

He turned his back to them and walked quickly to the exit.

He was furious.

* * *

Life was hell all week.

It was beyond everything to find himself in this situation. Suddenly, something was caving in. He lay in bed in the one-room he was renting by the week, feeling his heart beat hard, and his stomach sour.

Derek. Derek was always with him, like a painfully throbbing wound.

But there was a shred of dignity he had left, and it lay in his training. Self-discipline saved him.

He pulled himself out of bed, showered, shaved. He needed a haircut.

He put on fresh underwear, the same kind of khaki skivvies he always wore. But it wasn't the same any more. They were part of a uniform he wasn't allowed to wear anymore.

He had something to do. He had to go get a haircut and buy new underwear.

Chapter 3

Miracles Depend On Our Inner Resources.

That was what the sign said on the Unitarian Church signboard across the street from the bus depot.

Scotty Mason knew he needed one as he stood waiting for a bus at the terminal in a small town sixty miles outside Chicago. He had done his time as an army recruiter, and now he was going back east.

Sitting, drowsing, on the bus, watching great plains and the run-down industrial peripheries of small and large American cities pass by on the window screen he stared at, out of, through -- at himself.

In all those cities and towns, there for the eye to see, the infrastructures were crumbling.

He could feel it, because that's what it felt like inside himself. His infrastructure was crumbling, which once had been so shiny and new and strong.

How could his thoughts not carry him back to eighteen and Dartmouth and an overpowering sense of belonging and possessing? He had a right, then, to be everywhere. Everywhere he looked, it was his.

He relaxed into the memory and a warm sense of arousal flooded his body.

The earth smelled brown in the air and gladness was the smell the grass exuded. The early autumn of New England took him in her arms.

Darkness fell on the landscape and he fell fitfully asleep in his seat. Then he woke, not more refreshed, groggy, but now unable to re-enter distorted realms for a second sleep. He watched darkness stretch past him on the window glass.

And then he dozed, and then it was the gray dawn of New Jersey, and then it was the cold and cheerless Port Authority terminal.

He took his duffel bag from the bus's belly and walked away with it flung over his shoulder. He zipped up his wool-lined leather bomber jacket, and turned round 360 degrees looking at the signs for the one pointing to the Brooklyn subway.

A bunch of guys with skis milled around the newspaper stand. It was strange to be able to look at kids without having to figure out how to approach them. It was a relief. They were doing fine without him. They were looking good. He wanted nothing from anyone.

* * *

"It's really nice of you, Mike. I mean..."

"Oh, shut up Mason," he said taking the young man in his arms; "and come inside," he said, releasing him, but taking him around the waist again and leading him in.

"No," Mason, blushed, "I have to express to you how grateful I am that you could...do this."

Michael made a gesture that it was enough.

* * *

"You must be hungry."

"If I let myself feel it, yeah."

"But you don't?"

"Not much."

"Only with hunger?"

"Not only. No. Just about everything. Float gracefully above it."

"Otherwise?"

"Oh, I don't even go that far."

"Or get that near."

* * *

Michael's brownstone was on Fifth Avenue in Park Slope, a reviving neighborhood. But he had bought the house before the revival began. It had been in bad condition. Slowly, by himself and, when necessary, with outside help, he was redoing it. He hadn't paid much for it. He had managed to save enough from his nine years as an assistant professor of English at Dartmouth to make the down payment.

That's where Scott had met him. It was strange that they hit it off. They oughtn't to have.

Just like it shouldn't be Michael he turns to now. It doesn't make sense.

"It's been tough," Michael said, his hand on Scott's shoulder as he pours him a cup of herbal tea.

"Yeah!" Scott said, suddenly holding back tears.

"The pressure must have been immense."

Mason was silent.

Michael poured some tea for himself, replaced the kettle on the stove and sat facing him.

"You're welcome to stay here, as long as you need, as long as you want. There's plenty of room. I've made up a room for you on the third floor. It's in the middle of being redone, but it's habitable with a bed, a desk, a chair and a dresser. The radiator works and I put a rug down because the floors are unsanded. It'll be a good place to figure things out."

"I don't know how to thank you."

"It's ok. It's my pleasure to have you. So, thank you. Tell me are you still as reactionary politically as you always were?"

"What!" Mason smiled.

"You were a stubborn bastard."

"And you never seemed to mind."

"Ok, so tell me. What are your thoughts these days?"

"Truth is, Michael, I have no thoughts. Everything I stood on seems to have collapsed under me and now I can't tell if I'm swimming for my life or walking on air."

"Well you don't have to do either right now. You can just sit there."

"But I want to do so something. I mean, I'll get some money every month from the army. And I want to pay my share as long as I'm here. I don't want to be dependent."

"Might not be the worst thing for you if you could be openly dependent for a change."

"Openly?"

"Well, I know, you follow some party line that says we're each free and independent. But it just isn't so. You, for example, were stuck in the army, however much you might have wanted to be. You were forced to serve an interest that really was not yours, even if you thought it was. You were totally dependent! You were dependent on everyone. On the kids you were trying to recruit, on your superiors who could make your life miserable if you didn't meet quotas. How did you keep going this long without breaking down?"

Mason sipped his tea.

"But you know, Michael. I was interested. I wanted to know those kids. I wanted to do good by them. They're just hanging out at a mall with nothing to do. And I got a purpose for them that can turn their lives around."

"So that they'll be like yours."

"They are lost."

"And you?"

"So am I, I guess." He blushed. "But I would not have been lost if I could have found them. Hah! Looking for them, I got lost. I just expected they'd be there and that a uniform and your country meant something."

"But you were rejected?"

"Was I ever! Rejected! There was this one dude, you'd say, Derek. An industrial diamond ready to be fashioned into a precise instrument. I was on the brink with him. But I couldn't get in."

"And it stuck with you?"

"He stuck with me. It's a little bit like an obsession. I recognize that. But there it is. I want to see that fucker in uniform, standing at attention. I want to hear him cry out, 'Yes, sir.'"

Michael lifted his eyebrows.

"He certainly made an impression on you."

"I guess you keep thinking about the one that got away."

"Yup," Michael said standing. "Let me show you your room."

* * *

"Put simply, I don't know what to do with myself. I don't know who I am."

"What's the thing that bothered you the most about everything that happened?"

"I'm ashamed to say it, but not making a connection with that guy Derek."

"Oh but you did. You did more than that."

"Did what?"

"Make a connection."

"What do you mean?"

"I'm not sure I should tell you."

"Oh, come on, Michael. Don't play the guru with me."

"You made a connection with yourself..."

"With myself?"

"With yourself, through Derek."

"Through Derek?"

"Through Derek."

"With myself?"

"Because of Derek you got in touch with a part of yourself you don't want to allow. That's why you feel blank."

"Why?"

"Because you don't want to be who you are."

"What are you talking about?"

"You never did."

Chapter 4

"When's the last time you've lain in bed and held someone?"

"Lain?" Mason repeated laughing.

"Lain! When was the last time you've lain in bed and held somebody close to you?" Michael said.

"That's not a fair question."

"What's not fair about it?"

"It's personal."

"So?"

"So it's personal. People don't go around asking each other things like that."

"Oh, no. Right. But they do go around asking each other to go and kill somebody else or get killed themselves."

Scott Mason stared quietly at the ceiling as Michael lashed into him.

"What are you getting at, Michael?"

"No, it's what are you getting at, Scott? And how long is it going to take you to get there?"

"Why are you turning everything back on me? It's the same thing that Derek kid did. It makes me dizzy. I like things clear, plain, and simple."

"I wonder," Michael said. "But still the real question is what are you getting at? Where will this whole misadventure take you? Can you get yourself to the point where you can at least wonder that you were selling death to kids and then ask yourself how a decent guy like you could do a thing like that?"

But Mason blocked the question. Turning on his side, he said with a show of mild exasperation, "You still have the same left-wing slant you always have."

"It's not a left-wing slant." Michael glared. If he did not get through to him now, he never would and Mason would remain hopelessly broken, lost to himself, with no foundation.

"People with immense power and tremendous financial interest," he said with slow emphasis, "fight with each other for the control and ownership of this or that and they get one group of people scared of or angry at another group of people so that they're willing to bring death and grief to each other. That's what's really going on. No left-wing slant. The president lies. The secretary of defense lies. Cheney's got a dirty hand in everything. There's been a fucking coup d'état in the United States. And it's still going on. And there's a plague. Everything is being consumed by war and brutality, death and injury. People are scared of each other and are harming each other. And they're made to think and feel it's noble. Everybody has a good reason. And there's you out there in some suburb of Chicago trying to convince the kids to go to war, to become seriously maimed, to kill, to die, to torture for these people and their interests. Wow! Meanwhile, coincidentally, the whole infrastructure of the United States is falling apart, bigotry is being written into a constitutional amendment, major rights and freedoms are being threatened in the name of defending freedom, there's fucking torture, for Christ's sake, and the mainstream culture is getting stupider by the minute."

Mike stopped.

Slowly Scott drew in a breath. It was hot in the room. He was stretched out on his bed. Michael was in the arm-chair across from him. Scott knew what he was talking about. It was beating inside him like a caged animal he was frightened of.

Scott sat up. He pulled off his shirt.

"Go easy on me, Michael," he said, pressing his palms into his eyes.

"Sure, Scotty. I understand," Michael said. "I don't want to make it tough for you. But it's time you see things you haven't been able to."

Then Scott did a strange thing for him. He reached out his arm and offered his hand.

Michael took hold of it. Mason drew him to his bedside.

"Sit down," he said.

Michael sat beside Mason and Scott pressed his hand inside his own fist and brought it to his bare chest.

"I know, Michael. But you got to understand it isn't easy changing who you are."

"You don't have to change anything. You just have to accept...and everything will fall into place."

"To accept that I wanted those boys, especially Derek. And it excited me to..."

Michael waited.

But Mason veered suddenly from what he was going to say.

"You're queer for me?" Mason said, instead.

"I have always been," Michael responded quietly.

"But you never said anything."

"What's to say?"

"How you felt."

"I didn't have the right to do that."

"But what if I needed it?"

"You say that now after things have begun to be clear to you. But then, you would have run so fast. I wasn't interested in freaking you out but in keeping you steady."

"You were always so proper. I mean you were upfront about what you thought, but you were, I don't know, cold, like you had no feelings. I could not make it out. If you were friendly or what your motive was."

"I had no motive. Or if I did, it was to keep boys like you, decent kids but misguided, from signing away their souls and their bodies to the military. I wanted to make sure kids I taught got a sense that there were better things that they could do. That was my motive. With you, at the time, I failed. You were bull-headed, and you wanted something you could believe in and give yourself to."

"Instead of saying you were queer upfront, you insinuated yourself as a caring guru, but in the back of your mind, you were a seducer. You wanted us to think like you. It was your way of getting the feeling that you'd made a sexual conquest, that you existed, that you were important."

Michael looked at him quietly. Mason knew what he was thinking. It was true. He was talking about himself. It fit as perfectly as Cinderella's shoe.

"Seducer. Recruiter. What's the difference?" Scott muttered.

He held Michael's hand tighter and pressed it harder to his chest.

"Do you know what I did when I got home the day I met Derek?"

Michael looked waiting for him to tell him.

"I took off my uniform, looked at myself in the mirror, and jacked off thinking about Derek standing at attention in front of me saying, yes, sir to me."

At that point Mason broke down, but even in his softened condition he would not want us to watch him crying.

But we may talk about him when we are out of his presence and tell what discretion prevents us from showing.

It was not clear if Mason was crying at not being able to caress Derek or at realizing that he wanted to or, most likely, a ridiculous combination of the two.

Michael rocked him in his arms and put his cheek against his temple.

It made him sob more powerfully.

Michael held him tighter and felt Mason's tears on his own cheeks. He kissed his eyes gently. Mason tightened his grip on Michael and kissed the bend of his neck in response until their mouths slid together and met in a kiss that began tenderly and consolingly but soon became passionate.

Mason was lost in a sensation that was nothing like anything that he had known before.

"What have I been doing with my life?" he said, still crying, but softly, when he looked at Michael.

"What you had to do," Michael said, gently. "That's all. Welcome home."

The End

Here is a sample from another story you may enjoy:

Gideon Elliot

Sweet Surrender

TABOO BUNDLE

Gay Bondage Erotica

They met on St. Mark's Place outside The Taberna, a Greek place that Mark knew. It had begun to snow. They both arrived in front of the restaurant at the same time and embraced. No one had to wait outside in the cold for the other, stamping his feet.

"It's good to see you. I'm really sorry about last night," Mark said, a lovely smile gracing his face. But Tayler was not having it and told him he had nothing to apologize for although he might have a lot to think about.

"Like what?" Mark asked without rancor.

Tayler drew in his breath. "Like what you keep avoiding."

"What's that?"

"I don't know," Tayler said. "It just seems to me you are trying to blank something out."

You're so analytical," Mark said gently taking Tayler's cheeks in his palm and drawing his lips to him.

"Not here," Tayler said.

"And why not here?" Mark said.

"Look at your menu."

"Octopus."

"Octopus?"

"I like it," Mark said. "And vine leaves. They're good here."

So they both had a vinegar drenched grilled octopus and stuffed vine leaves and Tayler liked them. But he was easy to please, anyhow.

"Will you go with me next Friday night?" Mark said.

"You know what you're doing?"

"Yeah, being who I am. Openly, as they say."

Tayler shrugged. Outside, the snow had begun to fall again.

"Why else you want me to go?"

"Because I'm starting to feel like I need to be with you all the time. I'm complete only when I'm with you. Otherwise I'm missing something. Do you feel that way about me?"

"Do you think I'd surrender that kind of information to a sadist like you?"

"Torture will open your lips."

"So will kisses," Tayler said coming closer.

"In that case," Mark said, but the rest of his words were smothered in a kiss.

***

They were like two Greek warriors horsing around, wrestling with each other on the plains of Troy. Naked, their bodies glinted bronze in the evening light. They looked as if they were still clad in breastplates. As the blazing sun inched its orange-saturated ball downwards, it fell behind the distant jagged mountains. Then it became impossible to distinguish between rock and the ether.

They strained their muscles in the simultaneous effort to seize and to evade until the force of the power that strove through them brought their lips together and the kiss only intensified their struggle.

Tayler gave an open-throated yawn and squeezed Mark's hand as they walked through the chill air of Manhattan in December.

"I love you," Mark said.

"It's mutual," Tayler said. He meant it, but he was pessimistic. The surface often has a way of disappearing leaving you stuck somewhere that isn't anywhere. He looked at Mark.

"You don't believe me?" Mark said, stopping in his tracks and turning a full half circle so that he was facing him

"I don't know what to believe."

"Believe what I tell you."

"Yes, Sir," Tayler said with a grin, snapping to attention. Mark leaned over and the warm breath of his whisper taunted Tayler's neck. "I really mean it," he said.

"Time has a way of changing meaning," Tayler said with soft sadness in his voice. "And desire has a way of vanishing in time."

"Do you expect yours will?"

"I don't know."

They walked a little in silence until Tayler took Mark's hand. "Now it's my turn," he said, "to ask for forgiveness."

"For what?" Mark said, truly puzzled.

"For being a wet blanket."

"Wet as you are, I'd love to crawl under you. Come home with me. We can have some hot rum and you can fuck me. I'm starting to feel you inside me already." Tayler spotted a cab and hailed it. They sped through the city and got out in the urban pastoral of a snow-swept Washington Heights.

"I want it to be always like this," Mark said, his arm wrapped around Tayler's bare shoulder, looking into his eyes. Always."

Tayler nodded his head and smiled wistfully, fleetingly and then kissed Mark gently on the lips. He understood that he was committing himself to something that was sure to get out of his control.

If you enjoyed this sample then look for **Sweet Surrender**.

Also by this Author

A Second Chance

The Recruiter

A Furtive and Hidden Embrace

Diamond Shadows

Displacement

Keen Obedience

Between Two Thieves

Heart's Desire

Sensual Surrender

Erotic Aggression

Don't Forget You Love Me

Unstable Emotion

The Hazard Game

A Knight in the Forest

Captured Emotions

The Mesmerist's Tale

On His Own

The Good Bitch

Succumb Touch

Blue Identity

***

I REALLY LOVE Reviews!

If you enjoyed this book, please share the love and don't forget to leave a review on Amazon or the site of any other retailer you purchased this book from!

I highly appreciate your reviews, and it only takes a minute to write & post one. I can't tell you how much this means to me!

You'll find the list of all my books on my Author Central page... just in case you'd like to leave a review for other books of mine you've read but didn't have time to leave a review.

*Amazon Author Central – http://www.amazon.com/Gideon-Elliot/e/B00DUYBEQC

One Last Thing, For Kindle Readers...

When you turn the page, Kindle will give you the opportunity to rate this book and share your thoughts on Facebook and Twitter. If you enjoyed my writings, would you please take a few seconds to let your friends know about it? Because... when they enjoy they will be grateful to you and so will I.

Thank You!

Gideon Elliot
gideon_elliot@awesomeauthors.org

About the Author

Gideon Elliot was born in 1981 in Wichita, Kansas.

He grew up in San Francisco and spends the greater part of the year, now, on one of the Cyclades Islands in Greece where he runs a jazz café, paints, writes poetry, and swims.

He has a small apartment in Greenwich Village, where he stays from the middle of November to the end of April and, during those months, manages an erotic men's clothing shop. He began writing erotic fiction at the age of fifteen.

You may also like the books by these authors:

CHRIS**JOHNS**

BORDER
Patrol

HOT GAY EROTICA

Patrolling this sector of the border was fine during the spring and summer months. Even in the autumn it was still pleasant, but now, in the winter, it was miserable. The choice appeared to be snow or rain, and always cold.

The patrols were on foot because the forest was too dense for vehicles and of course they were too noisy. The actual border had a fence and a road alongside it, but the commander thought roving foot patrols about a kilometre inside the border would catch more illegals because they would be less careful, now that they were across into Germany. Unfortunately he was proved correct. The patrols along the border road were always finding holes in the fence, but seldom caught anyone. But Heinrich and Jorge had captured hundreds in the year they had been doing it. On one wall in the small compound where they took the captured illegals they had rows of little men, indicating the number they had been able to return to Poland. They had started it as a joke.

"Just like our Luftwaffe Pilots marked their kills on the sides of their aircraft during the war," Jorge had said when they started it.

There was another separate tally in a notebook Jorge kept in his locker. That was the number they had not declared, always the young pretty ones or the just plain sexy. The two young guards were gay and would on occasions, when they captured a particularly attractive guy, offer him his freedom in return for sexual favors. It was fun and in the winter lightened up an otherwise dull down time. They were never refused. The young ones particularly would have sold their soul to be allowed into the West so there was never any forced sexual contact; the detainees were offered a simple choice. After they had been stripped and scoped out thoroughly the offer would be made.

"If you look as sexy when your penis is erect as you do now with it flaccid we will let you go, but not until after we have checked how good you can blow us and take our cocks up your arse."

Some were quite enthusiastic, others were very resentful but most just accepted it as the price for their freedom.

Petrov was one of the resentful ones, but he had such a superb slim body that Jorge wanted to keep him for days.

"He will get used to it, and then he will enjoy my cock up his arse. If he becomes very good I might keep him in my apartment in Hamburg as a permanent sex toy for use during my time off."

Heinrich had laughed. He and Jorge had been friends since joining the army at eighteen, and had stayed together during their military service, joining the border patrol unit when they had served their enlisted time. The pay was good, the time off was brilliant so despite the rotten hours when they were on duty and the miserable weather in the winter they had stayed. Jorge was the joker and Heinrich loved him like a brother.

The capture of Petrov had been standard. The snow made it so easy to follow the illegals. They stopped covering their tracks about 100 metres inside the border. With their snowshoes on, Heinrich and Jorge could move much faster than the prey over the loose snow so even if they were seen early it didn't matter, the chase just lasted a little longer.

A pistol held to his temple while Jorge cuffed him and fixed a lead to the cuffs soon had him resigned to his fate and he followed without any more trouble. Once inside the accommodation he was released from his restraints and told to strip. No trouble, there seldom was, once caught they knew there was no point in fighting it. They would of course serve time in a prison at home, but then they would try again.

Jorge had a good digital camera, the same as the official one. When Petrov was naked, he took only ones for his private collection. The encrypted files on his computer were a gallery of gorgeous naked Polish boys, many of them with erections. They showed gorgeous cocks and cute butts that Jorge knew he was going to slide his cock into.

When Petrov was naked, Heinrich carried out a body search, making it as humiliating as possible to subdue any thoughts of objection at a later stage.

"Spread your legs and bend over the desk, I am going to check that you are not secreting drugs on your person."

As he was talking, Heinrich was plastering one hand with a lubricant while Jorge had his revolver out ready to use. The humiliation was easy, a slow increase in the number of fingers being used to finger fuck him.

"This one has a really cute butt Jorge, your cock will think it has gone to heaven if you slide in here."

Jorge laughed and got the camera ready when he realized Petrov was not going to fight.

Using his own camera he took full length front and back. What he was faced with was a tall early 20's Polish man. He was slim built with fine muscle definition, slim waist and a gorgeous arse. Jorge could hardly contain himself, he so wanted to cup those two perfect little cheeks in his hands and then spread them so that he could see his little rosebud. Short, black hair, almost black eyes and long, but well-proportioned face made for a very sexy picture.

Petrov

"You are a very sexy looking man Petrov. If you get an erection and we still like what we see, you will be invited to suck our cocks. Then we will see how good it feels to slide them into your arse. When we have enjoyed your body fully, we will let you go provided you never mention that you were captured if you are ever caught by the authorities."

The boy was obviously thinking about this, was it worth being buggered to get into Germany, and if he allowed it, would they keep their word? The risks he had already taken to get this far made him shudder, and he really didn't want to go to a prison in his motherland, they were quite grim.

Acquiesce and put it behind him when it was finished. He took his hands away from his groin and started to play with himself. When he was erect he dropped his hands to his sides and looked at his captors.

"Oh my God, Heinrich, I don't know about him sucking me, I know I am going down on him as soon as we have showered."

Petrov was surprised and pleased that whatever they were going to do to him, and make him do to them it was going to be with clean bodies. He was badly in need of this shower; he had been running and hiding for days as he approached the border. It would be heaven to be clean again.

Heinrich remained clothed and ready for action as he watched Jorge thoroughly pamper Petrov in the showers.

"This will warm you up Petrov. I can see you are still cold from your exposure. My name is Jorge and I am going to take my time to make love to you. I think you are a very sexy man."

Petrov was confused, he was expecting to be raped and humiliated, not pampered and made love to.

"How old are you?"

Petrov told him. "I am 21, Jorge." He said the name hesitantly which made Jorge laugh.

"I am 21 as well, we should be friends."

Petrov relaxed, and as he did so he took in more of this young German who was now being so nice to him. Jorge was bigger than Petrov in build, he also had a big penis which Petrov could see clearly now, and it was bigger than his. The thought of being fucked by it was not the most thrilling, but perhaps it wouldn't hurt too much if Jorge was gentle with him.

"Have you ever played with boys sexually, Petrov?"

The Pole shook his head.

"Well, I am going to have lots of fun teaching you how to pleasure me and I will do that by pleasuring you."

Jorge was thoroughly enjoying this. Petrov looked quite fierce but he was proving to be a little darling. He was gently spoken and appeared to have accepted his lot. His German was very good as well. Jorge thought he would probably meld in quite well with the German people. He was of course black haired so not a true Aryan, but lots of Germans were as well with all the interbreeding that had gone on since the war.

Jorge thoroughly soaped Petrov's body before gently fondling his cock and balls. It felt so good. The cock was very hard but the ball sac still had enough play in it to please Jorge. The Pole was clearly excited by all this attention and made no objection when Jorge told him to turn round. The butt was exquisite and Jorge couldn't resist moving in close so that his cock was lodged in the crack between the perfect little cheeks.

"You feel so good, and look so exciting. I know I am going to take you to Paradise."

The feel of another man's cock sliding up and down between his cheeks should have upset him, but Petrov realized he was enjoying it. Jorge continued to play with him and stroke him until he thought he would orgasm if it went on.

"I am almost ready to cum Jorge, you excite me so much."

Jorge was so pleased. He turned Petrov back round, made sure that both of them were free of soap and then dropped to his knees and took Petrov's cock into his mouth. Just a few inches so that he could swab the glans with his tongue. Too much for Petrov after all the stimulation, he came almost immediately and was horrified that Jorge had no time to pull off. The horror turned to surprise when he realized that Jorge was sucking him gently, taking all his cum as he went soft.

"Mmm, that tasted so good, I think I am going to want to do that again before we release you."

He stood up then, took Petrov in his arms and kissed him softly on the lips. This was amazing, Petrov didn't know what to do or say. He loved everything this German guard was doing to him.

Jorge

Heinrich was watching all of this and was as amazed as Petrov at his friend's actions. They had been together for years, and in this job for over a year and he had never seen Jorge show such affection for a detainee. Usually it was a suck and fuck before throwing them out, but here he was pampering this one in the shower and going down on him, and then kissing him. What on earth was going on?

When Jorge took Petrov through to the sleeping quarters instead of just fucking him over the desk, Heinrich knew it was time to step in.

"Jorge, this boy is just a fuck, he isn't your new boyfriend."

Jorge blushed a deep red as he looked at his friend. "I'm sorry Heinrich. I have feelings for this man that I have never had for any of the other detainees. I want to make love to him, not just rape him. I know I have to let you have a go as well, but please, be gentle with him when it is your turn."

If you enjoyed this sample then look for **Border Patrol**.

OWNED
in SINGAPORE

GAY SUBMISSION EROTICA

DEXTER CHASE

"Alex, come in, sit down. Coffee?"

Alexander Dupree did as he was told and thanked his boss. "Black with two, please, Sir."

He was very wary as to why he was being talked to in such a friendly manner. His performance to date had earned him two warning letters. The next time it would be dismissal, and the last thing Alex could afford at the present time was the sack.

"I'm sure you are aware that your performance this year has been well below what we have come to expect from you. Two years ago you were on track to make partner. Then, a little less than a year ago it all started to unravel for you. We have been very disappointed because we saw you as the future. You were our senior associate, and the youngest. I have talked to the other partners and we have made a decision concerning your future."

Alex took the coffee offered to him as his boss spoke. Was this the big push being built up to by giving him all the reasons for it? He knew he had been underperforming. During his first two years with the partnership he had closed so many difficult deals he had become something of a legend. He was only 26, single and considered a premium catch for any female. His apartment in the centre of town was furnished in the height of good taste and luxury, his BMW convertible was less than two years old. His level of debt was frightening.

The boss sat back down behind his desk and looked hard at his fallen star.

"I am sure you are aware that our best efforts to secure the deal with Straits Technical have not borne fruit. We think that in your hay day you would have tied this up with little effort so we are giving you a last chance to prove yourself. We are sending you to Singapore to replace Jason Oakley on the negotiating team. He will remain to assist you, but this will be your deal to make or lose. If you bring the deal back we will tear up your two written warnings, re-instate you as senior associate and guarantee you a partnership in twelve months if you then continue to perform the way you did before the drop in standards."

Alex knew he could do it if he could just get over his feeling of loss at his poor performance. He had no idea why he had lost it, but after the first written warning he got depressed and his underperformance accelerated. If he could start again he knew he would be ok. The pressure to succeed where everyone else had failed just acted as a challenge to him now.

"Thank you, Sir. I won't let you down."

"We hope not, Alex. We don't want to lose you but we need results to be better than your last year has produced."

Coffee finished, detailed folder presented to him.

"Take that away and absorb it. Be ready to leave for Singapore after the weekend."

That was it. Alex spent the weekend absorbing the contents of the folder. He spoke to Jason Oakley for hours getting all the personal details of the negotiating team from Singapore Technical. It was his ability to get the opposing negotiating teams onside that had been his greatest asset, now he needed it again, big time.

Monday morning, a first class seat on Singapore Airways and he was on his way. He was so pleased he could link his laptop to a power source because virtually the whole of the flight he was working on it. Jason met him at Changi and whisked him away to his hotel.

"We are going in for another round of talks after lunch, Alex. Do you want to sit in or have a rest and start fresh tomorrow?"

"I'll sit in, Jason. Introduce me to the other team and I'll just observe today. Conference with our team tonight and then I'll take over tomorrow morning."

Jason had mixed feelings being replaced by this much younger man who he knew had failed to shine the last twelve months.

"Very well, Alex. I'll give you all the support I can, but believe me, you will need a miracle to get Phillip Chen to go down our road in this deal."

"But he is only one man, what about the others?"

"The others are lackeys. They just say what Phillip tells them to. If you crack him you have the deal, but none of us have been able to."

During the afternoon sitting, Alex observed Phillip Chen closely, not missed by Phillip himself. Phillip had noticed Alex for different reasons to what should have been expected.

By the time Alex went to bed that night, despite the 8 hour time zone change, he slept like a baby, completely wiped out, but confident he had a handle on this whole deal, ready to do battle.

If you enjoyed this sample then look for **Owned in Singapore**.

GAY ROMANCE

Be My
One and Only

ERIK HESLOVE

Raconteur

In the beginning, they usually visit very often. They come weeping, with flowers and sit for hours at their loved one's grave, talking to the headstones, reminiscing. That doesn't last long though, soon the spaces between visits grow larger and eventually they stop for years.

This one was a fresh one; the corpse must still be decaying. She stood up after placing the most loving of kisses on the head stone and then looked ahead of herself. Ha, she wouldn't be kissing his lips if she could, not with all the dirt and festering flesh, oozing liquids and worms coming out of the poor bastard's mouth by now. The woman stared for a while, definitely in grief, at nothing in particular, a tree before her, behind the grave stone.

Everyone who visited stared at it. Even at the funerals, they noticed it. Some looked up and smiled as if something had been confirmed, others were confused. This woman shook her head and laughed lightly, through tears and sorrow, she managed a laugh. She was not like the other visitor, wife of the other deceased, who came by once in a while, left the flowers, spent a few minutes and then went back to a perfect life. You could tell the other visitor's life was perfect, always looked great, and barely ever fell into tears.

No, this one usually brought flowers for both graves, and would often spend time taking care of both. It was a tragic story, I didn't know much, I hear a lot about tragic deaths being a grave digger . . . but this one was one of the worst, the deaths being so intimately related and one after the other. That tree was special. It was the carving on it, and that it stood above the grave, a special place for sure.

If you enjoyed this sample then look for Be My One and Only.

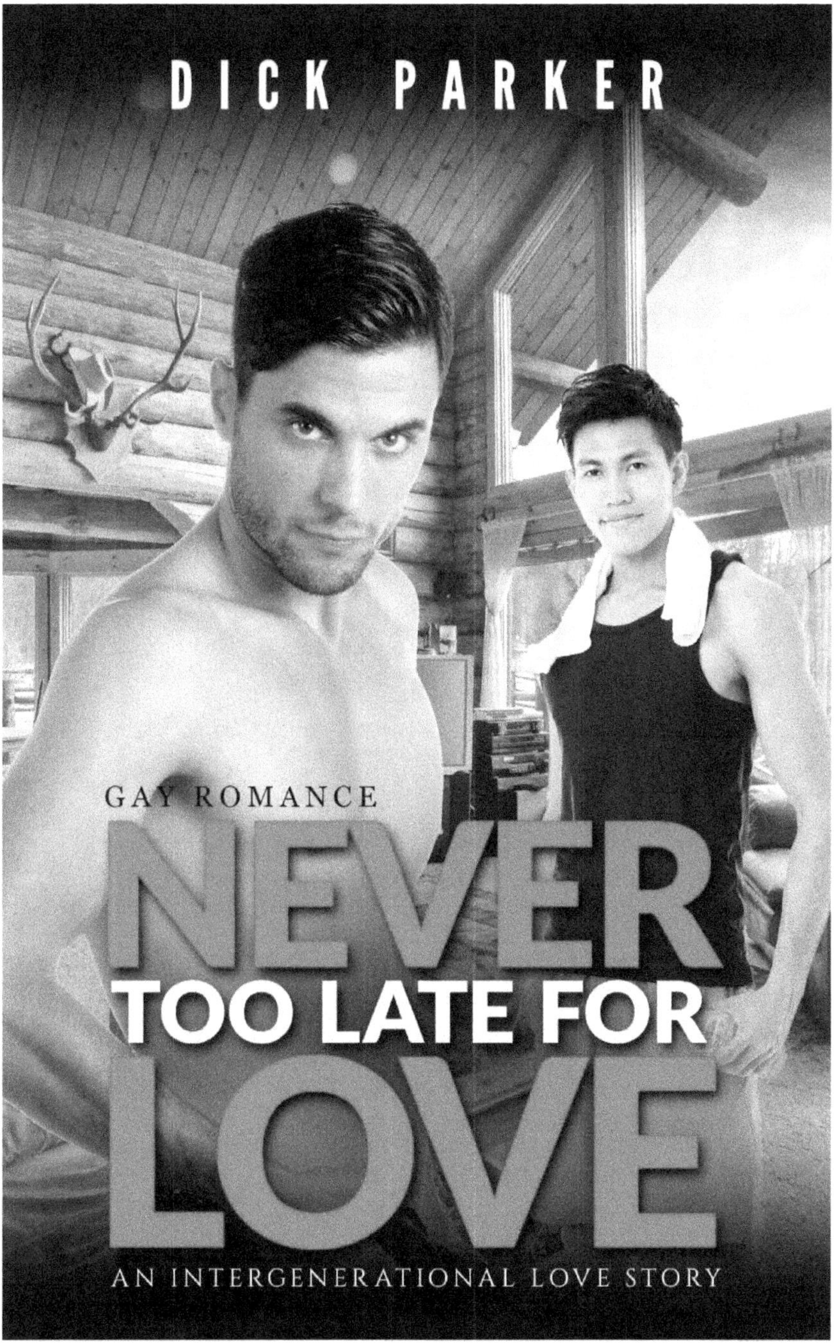
DICK PARKER
GAY ROMANCE
NEVER
TOO LATE FOR
LOVE
AN INTERGENERATIONAL LOVE STORY

"Do you have an appointment?"

"I've never been in a massage place before," I said. "I didn't know I needed one."

"Most of the time we need appointments. But we had a cancellation and I could fit you in. That is, if you don't mind being massaged by another man."

I hadn't expected that but actually it kind of made me feel more comfortable. "That's fine," I said.

She went back behind a curtain and a minute later she came back followed by a boy. He was beautiful. He looked like he was part Asian and maybe part Hispanic. He was small but very well built with smooth dark skin, shiny black hair and brown eyes. His face was angelic. He smiled at me and his smile was beautiful.

"This is Tran."

I nodded to the kid. "I'm Charlie. Charlie Dodge," I said.

"The fee is $50 for one half hour. If you are satisfied you may tip your masseur," the woman said.

I handed her $50.

"Please follow me, Mr. Dodge," the kid said.

He was wearing black silk shorts and a white strap undershirt and flip-flops. I guessed him at about five-foot five and maybe a hundred twenty pounds. His hair was longish and cut in a boyish style that hung over his ears and down his back a bit. He had bangs in front.

I followed him and took a good look at his cute ass. Damn the kid had a hell of an ass on him. He was cute as hell but way too young. We went in a little room with a waist- high narrow bed that was covered with a thin mat and a sheet. There was a table with oils and things on it and a stack of towels.

"Would you like me to step out while you undress?" he asked.

"I have to get completely naked?"

"Only if you choose. What part of your body do you wish to have worked on?"

I explained about my side and shoulder.

"You may keep your pants on if you wish. You would probably be more comfortable without them, but it is your choice."

I thought about it for a second. What the hell? How often did I get a chance to get naked in front of a hot little shit like this?

I took off my shirt, and shoes and socks. Then I dropped my jeans and boxers and stepped out of them. He looked. But then he patted the bed and I lay on it flat on my stomach. He put a little towel over my ass. He traced his fingers over my scar. It ran from my shoulder blade down about nine inches to my side.

"What happened?" he asked.

I explained the surgery.

"They opened your lung?"

"I was a sick man."

"Is it very painful? I am afraid to touch it."

"The scar is fine. It's down under where it hurts. They cut some ribs and then put in a thing they called a spreader. It's like a device that they crank open so they can get their hands in there to work on me. The spreader crushed all the nerves and muscles and tendons. That's why I'm so sore."

"I will be very careful."

He put some warm oil on my back and I felt his soft hands touching me. He lightly worked on the area and it felt really nice. "Am I hurting you?"

"No it feels nice. You can do it a bit harder if you want."

He worked the place harder. It gave me a twinge of pain now and then, but it really felt nice most of the time. "You have wonderful hands, Tran."

"Thank you, Mr. Dodge."

"Call me Charlie."

"Yes, Mr. Charlie."

I laughed.

He worked me for quite a while. Then I started getting a little sore from the muscles being rubbed.

"I think that's enough for today," I said.

"You still have ten minutes left of time."

"Well, that's okay," I said.

"I could do your shoulders and back. You feel tense."

"Sure," I said.

He put oil on my shoulders and back and began massaging them. Oh man, the kid knew what he was doing. He squeezed and rubbed and it felt amazing. Then he moved down and did my legs. He was working on the back of my thighs next. Damn, his hands were like warm butter. His hands were up on the top of my thighs and then where they moved to turned into butt.

"Would you like me to go a bit higher?"

Oh man.

"If I have time left, sure."

He took the towel off my ass. He put a little oil on my ass cheeks and kneaded them like two balls of bread dough. Damn, it felt good… and I started getting a hard-on.

"I think that's enough, Tran," I said.

"Let me wipe the oil off," he said.

He took a towel and wiped me down. Then he said I could get up. I had a semi-boner so I tried to keep my back to him. He put the towel in a hamper and when he turned back he looked at my half-hard cock.

If you enjoyed this sample then look for **Never Too Late For Love**.

AMY REDEK

His SPECIAL LESSONS

Quentin College was a place that I had taken a fancy to when I was studying for my doctorate at University and was very pleased when I received a letter asking me to attend an interview. I was one of twenty there that day and I progressed into the next interview of ten and finally for a third visit of just three of us for a position in such a prestigious college.

I was the last to be interviewed and I went into the Dean's office to find two other people sitting there along with the Dean himself, who had been present at my two previous visits. He was sitting behind his large desk and flanked by a man on his right and a woman on his left. I knew of them through my studies and the newspapers but waited until I was formally introduced to them before speaking.

'Sit down, Dr. Smith,' Dean Ainsworth said, indicating the chair placed before the desk. 'I am pleased to see that you made it to the last three and through your work, I'm sure you know Mrs. Cynthia Carrington who is attached to the Department of Education in the present government.' I nodded in her direction and gave her a small smile. 'And Sir Reginald Hudson, who, though in opposition at the moment, is the Chairman of the College Board of Governors.' I nodded in his direction and gave him the same smile.

'To recap for their benefit, you were born on the 14th May 1974 in London, christened Colin Franklin Smith and are now twenty-six years of age with both parents now deceased. You won high honours at college and obtained your doctorate at Oxford in the field of Political History on a brilliant thesis showing the parallels between the English Civil War and the American war of Independence. You have also written a book using these lines, which I myself have read and have ordered copies for the college library.

Now having seen you twice previously, I'll let my esteemed colleagues put forward their questions as to why you think you are fit for the position in this college. Mrs. Carrington, if you would be so kind as to lead off.'

He sat back with a smile on his face and listened to the questions that were fired at me for over half an hour and to my answers. They were very demanding and I gave the best answers that I could and felt mentally drained when it was over and shook hands all round before I left, being told that I would be notified within a week if I'd succeeded to the post or not.

I went back to London to my home in Chelsea. A house in Cheyne Walk left to me by my parents two years ago. My father had been a cardiac consultant, but his profession did nothing for him for he died of a heart attack at the age of sixty-one. Mother, with his loss, just seemed to pine away and so followed him two years later, but it was recorded as natural causes in her case.

That was two and a half years ago and so I went off to America to further my education in my field and had only been back in England for three months before applying for this doctorate post of Political History at Quentin College. In the States, I had attended Yale University, and by having the other side of the story as it were about what led up to the War of Independence, prompted me to write my thesis.

True to their word, I received a letter a week after my last interview from Dean Ainsworth congratulating me on securing the post and could take up residence whenever I wished for the incumbent had already retired. It was two weeks into the summer holidays and another four weeks before the new term year began; and as I didn't have any ties, immediately packed all that I would need and set off for the college.

Before the taxi driver could even begin to grumble about helping me get my two trunks down to his cab, I gave him a fiver and then had him drive me to the station where I had to get a porter to get them to my platform. The train I wanted was there and people were already boarding and I just had enough time to get my ticket and see the trunks put into the guards van.

If you enjoyed this sample then look for **His Special Lessons**.

WANT FREE COPIES OF MY BOOKS?

Just visit my blog and download free copies of my books:
http://gideon-elliot.awesomeauthors.org/gideon-elliot/

www.ingramcontent.com/pod-product-compliance
Lightning Source LLC
Chambersburg PA
CBHW071344130626
46556CB00005B/2023